MARVELOUS LAND OF OZ

VOL. 6

ADAPTED FROM THE NOVEL BY L. FRANK BAUM

Writer: ERIC SHANOWER
Artist: SKOTTIE YOUNG
Colorist: JEAN-FRANCOIS BEAULIEU
Letterer: JEFF ECKLEBERRY

Assistant Editor: MICHAEL HORWITZ
Editor: NATE COSBY

Collection Editor: MARK D. BEAZLEY
Assistant Editors: ALEX STARBUCK & NELSON RIBEIRO
Editor, Special Projects: JENNIFER GRÜNWALD
Senior Editor, Special Projects: JEFF YOUNGQUIST
SVP of Print & Digital Publishing Sales: DAVID GABRIEL
Production: JERRY KALINOWSKI
Book Design: ARLENE SO

Editor in Chief: AXEL ALONSO
Chief Creative Officer: JOE QUESADA
Publisher: DAN BUCKLEY
Executive Producer: ALAN FINE

Spotlight   **MARVEL**

visit us at www.abdopublishing.com

Reinforced library bound edition published in 2014 by Spotlight, a division of
the ABDO Group, PO Box 398166, Minneapolis, Minnesota 55439. Spotlight
produces high-quality reinforced library bound editions for schools and libraries.
Published by agreement with Marvel Characters, Inc.

Printed in the United States of America, North Mankato, Minnesota.
102013
012014
♻ This book contains at least 10% recycled materials.

Marvel.com
© 2014 Marvel

Library of Congress Cataloging-in-Publication Data

Shanower, Eric.
  The marvelous land of Oz / adapted from the novel by L. Frank Baum ; writer:
Eric Shanower ; artist: Skottie Young. -- Reinforced library bound edition.
      pages cm
  "Marvel."
  Summary: When the Scarecrow, now the ruler of the Emerald City, is driven
out by General Jinjur and her all-girl army, his friends--the Tin Woodman, a boy
named Tip, and Jack Pumpkinhead--try to restore peace in this graphic novel ad-
aptation of L. Frank Baum's classic tale.
  ISBN 978-1-61479-235-2 (vol. 1) -- ISBN 978-1-61479-236-9 (vol. 2) -- ISBN
978-1-61479-237-6 (vol. 3) -- ISBN 978-1-61479-238-3 (vol. 4) -- ISBN 978-1-
61479-239-0 (vol. 5) -- ISBN 978-1-61479-240-6 (vol. 6) -- ISBN 978-1-61479-
241-3 (vol. 7) -- ISBN 978-1-61479-242-0 (vol. 8)
  1. Graphic novels. [1. Graphic novels. 2. Fantasy.] I. Young, Skottie, illustrator.
II. Baum, L. Frank (Lyman Frank), 1856-1919. Marvelous land of Oz. III. Title.
  PZ7.7.S453Mar 2014
  741.5'973--dc23
                            2013030127

All Spotlight books are reinforced library binding
and manufactured in the United States of America.

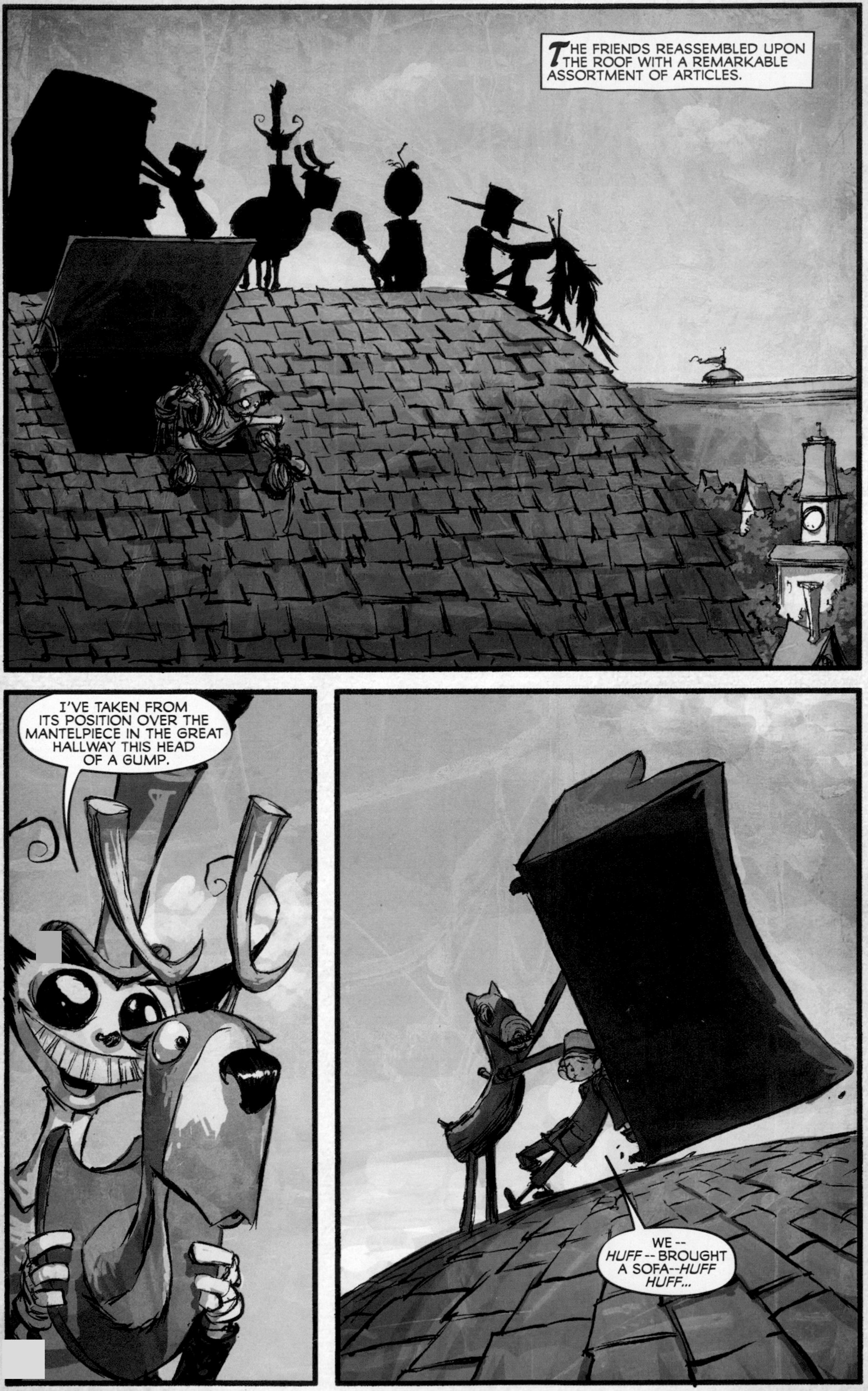
THE FRIENDS REASSEMBLED UPON THE ROOF WITH A REMARKABLE ASSORTMENT OF ARTICLES.
I'VE TAKEN FROM ITS POSITION OVER THE MANTELPIECE IN THE GREAT HALLWAY THIS HEAD OF A GUMP.
WE -- *HUFF* -- BROUGHT A SOFA--*HUFF HUFF*...

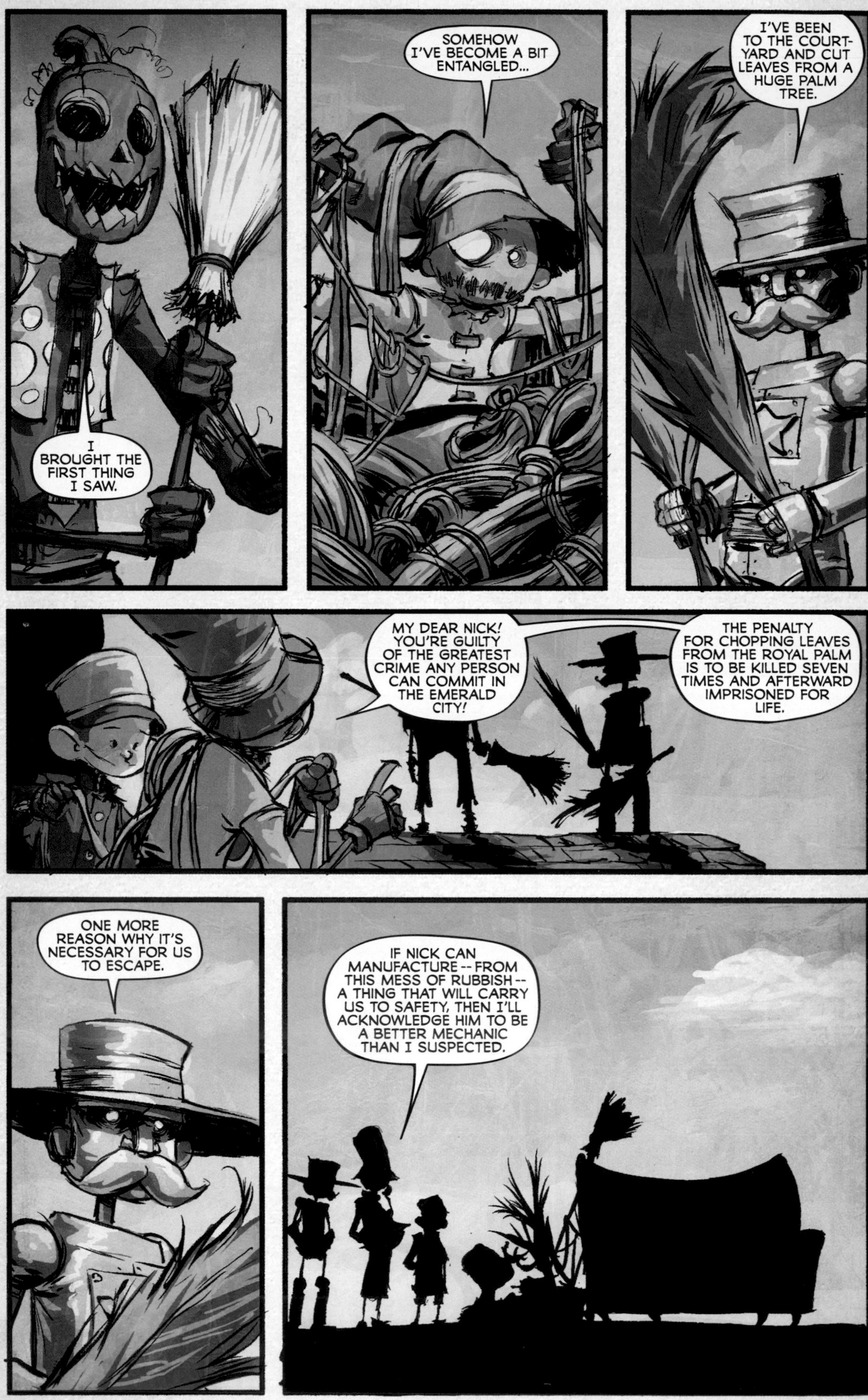
I BROUGHT THE FIRST THING I SAW.
SOMEHOW I'VE BECOME A BIT ENTANGLED...
I'VE BEEN TO THE COURT-YARD AND CUT LEAVES FROM A HUGE PALM TREE.
MY DEAR NICK! YOU'RE GUILTY OF THE GREATEST CRIME ANY PERSON CAN COMMIT IN THE EMERALD CITY!
THE PENALTY FOR CHOPPING LEAVES FROM THE ROYAL PALM IS TO BE KILLED SEVEN TIMES AND AFTERWARD IMPRISONED FOR LIFE.
ONE MORE REASON WHY IT'S NECESSARY FOR US TO ESCAPE.
IF NICK CAN MANUFACTURE -- FROM THIS MESS OF RUBBISH -- A THING THAT WILL CARRY US TO SAFETY, THEN I'LL ACKNOWLEDGE HIM TO BE A BETTER MECHANIC THAN I SUSPECTED.

THE FIRST THING REQUIRED IS A BODY BIG ENOUGH TO CARRY THE ENTIRE PARTY.

THIS SOFA MIGHT BE USED FOR A BODY, BUT SHOULD THE MACHINE EVER TIP SIDEWAYS, WE'D ALL SLIDE OFF.

WHY NOT USE TWO SOFAS? THERE'S ANOTHER ONE JUST LIKE THIS DOWNSTAIRS.

THAT'S A VERY SENSIBLE SUGGESTION.

*T*IP AND THE SAW-HORSE MANAGED TO GET THE SECOND SOFA TO THE ROOF.

EXCELLENT! WE CAN RIDE WITHIN THIS SNUG NEST QUITE AT OUR EASE.

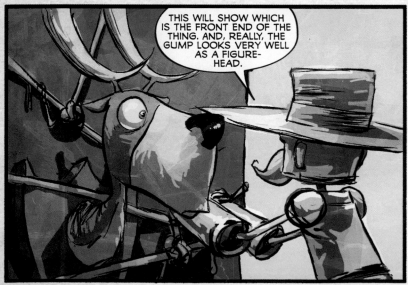

THIS WILL SHOW WHICH IS THE FRONT END OF THE THING. AND, REALLY, THE GUMP LOOKS VERY WELL AS A FIGURE-HEAD.

THESE GREAT PALM LEAVES -- FOR WHICH I'VE ENDANGERED MY LIFE SEVEN TIMES -- MUST SERVE US AS WINGS.

ARE THEY STRONG ENOUGH?

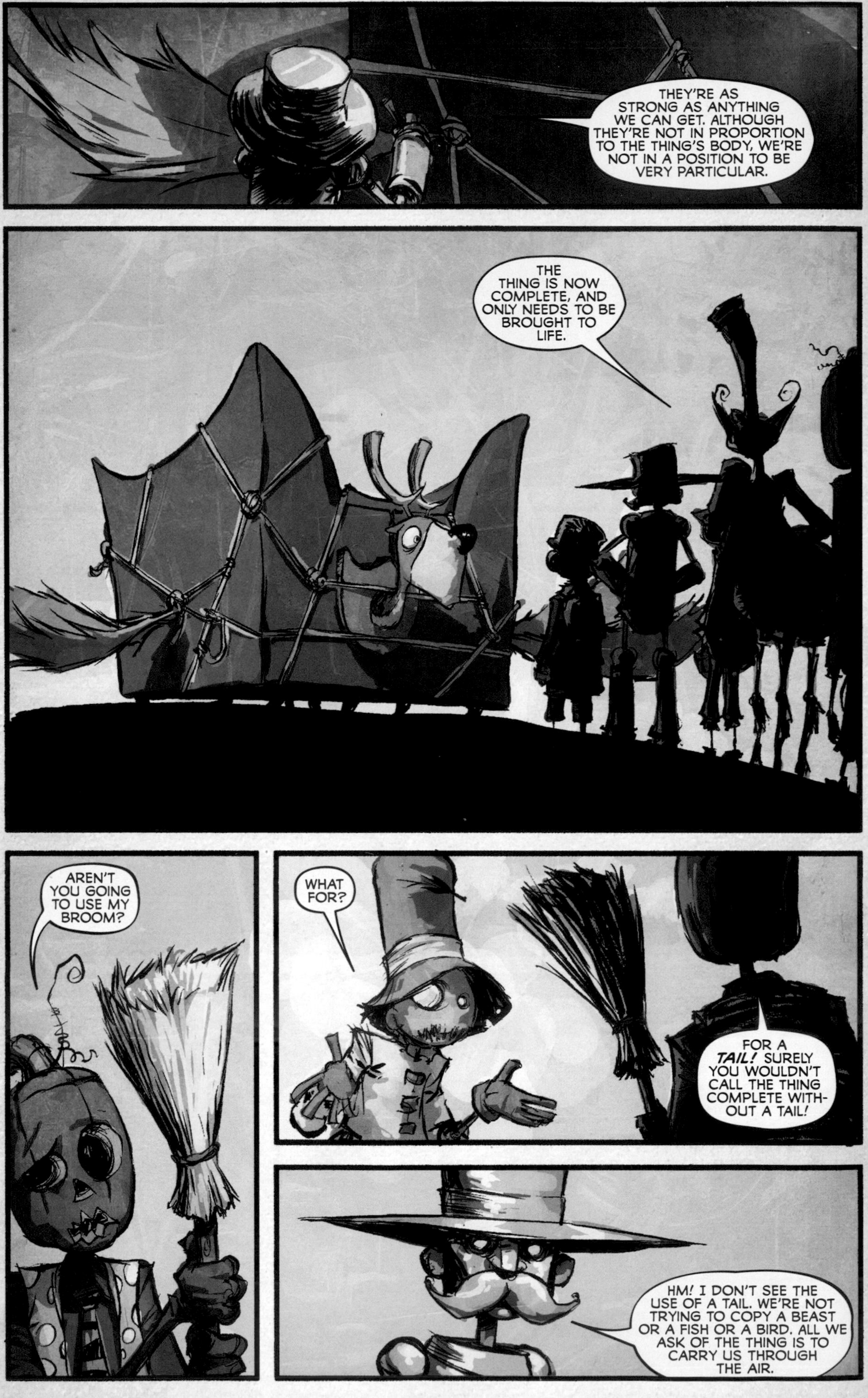
THEY'RE AS STRONG AS ANYTHING WE CAN GET. ALTHOUGH THEY'RE NOT IN PROPORTION TO THE THING'S BODY, WE'RE NOT IN A POSITION TO BE VERY PARTICULAR.
THE THING IS NOW COMPLETE, AND ONLY NEEDS TO BE BROUGHT TO LIFE.
AREN'T YOU GOING TO USE MY BROOM?
WHAT FOR?
FOR A *TAIL!* SURELY YOU WOULDN'T CALL THE THING COMPLETE WITH-OUT A TAIL!
HM! I DON'T SEE THE USE OF A TAIL. WE'RE NOT TRYING TO COPY A BEAST OR A FISH OR A BIRD. ALL WE ASK OF THE THING IS TO CARRY US THROUGH THE AIR.

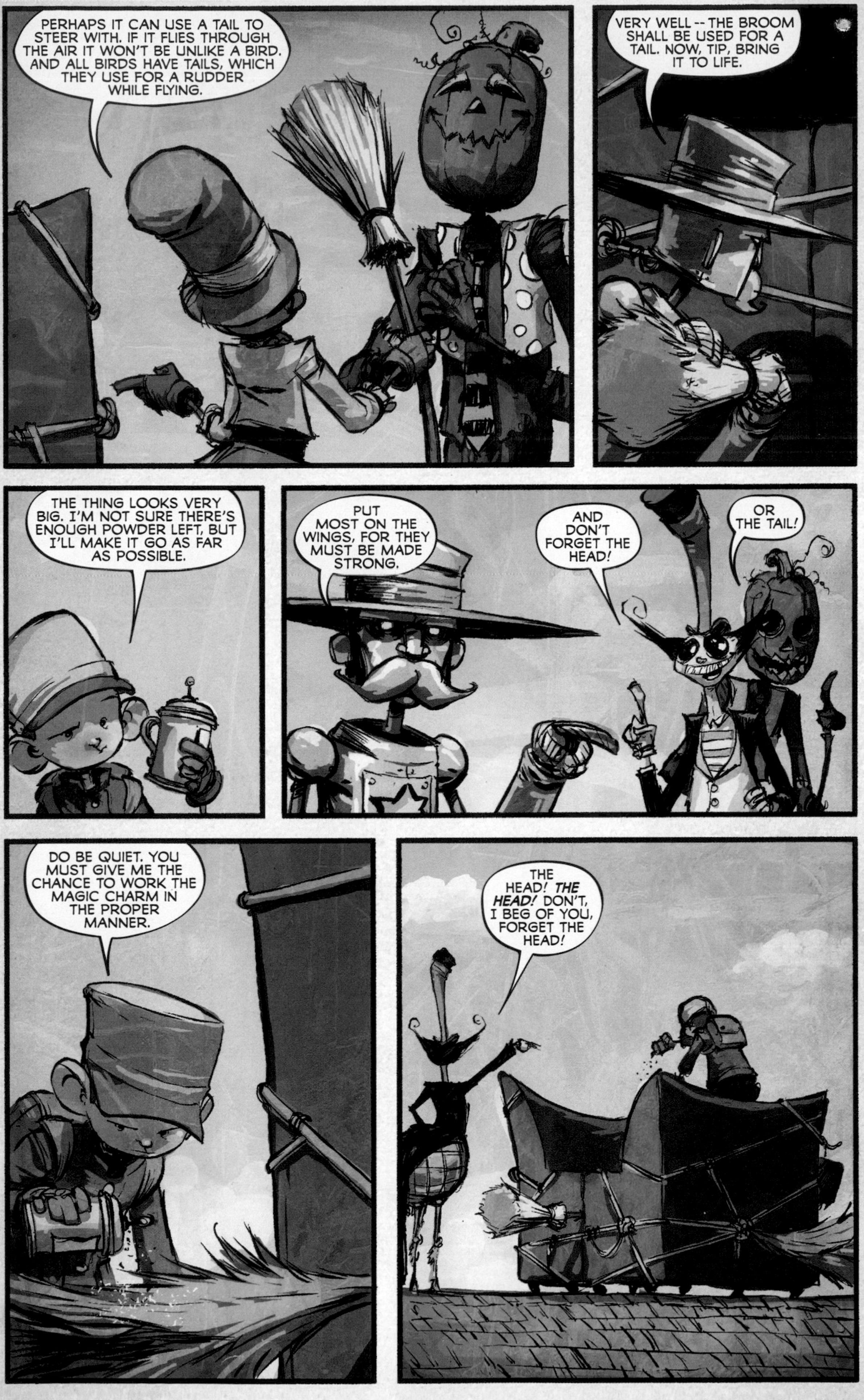
PERHAPS IT CAN USE A TAIL TO STEER WITH. IF IT FLIES THROUGH THE AIR IT WON'T BE UNLIKE A BIRD. AND ALL BIRDS HAVE TAILS, WHICH THEY USE FOR A RUDDER WHILE FLYING.
VERY WELL -- THE BROOM SHALL BE USED FOR A TAIL. NOW, TIP, BRING IT TO LIFE.
THE THING LOOKS VERY BIG. I'M NOT SURE THERE'S ENOUGH POWDER LEFT, BUT I'LL MAKE IT GO AS FAR AS POSSIBLE.
PUT MOST ON THE WINGS, FOR THEY MUST BE MADE STRONG.
AND DON'T FORGET THE HEAD!
OR THE TAIL!
DO BE QUIET. YOU MUST GIVE ME THE CHANCE TO WORK THE MAGIC CHARM IN THE PROPER MANNER.
THE HEAD! *THE HEAD!* DON'T, I BEG OF YOU, FORGET THE HEAD!

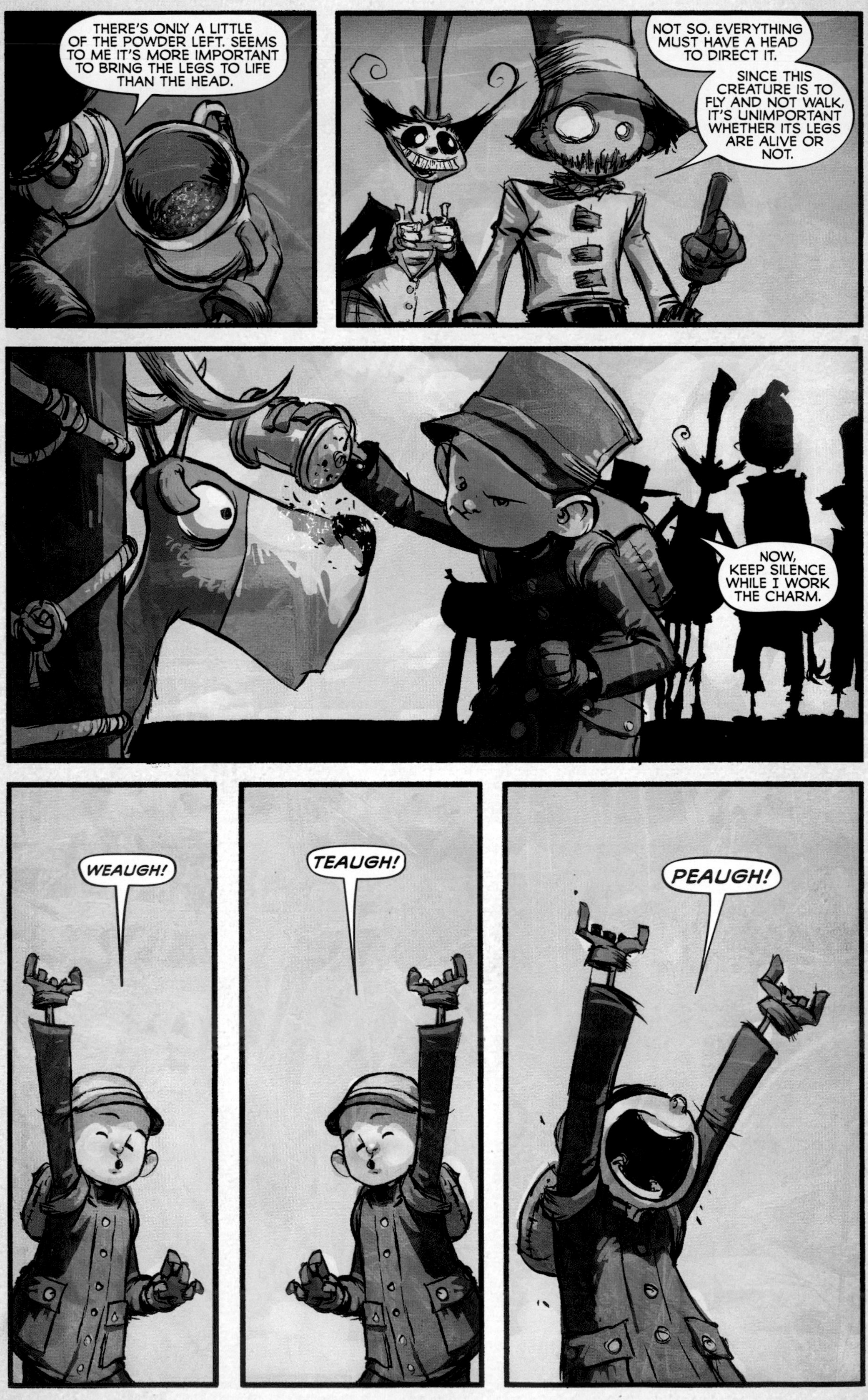
THERE'S ONLY A LITTLE OF THE POWDER LEFT. SEEMS TO ME IT'S MORE IMPORTANT TO BRING THE LEGS TO LIFE THAN THE HEAD.
NOT SO. EVERYTHING MUST HAVE A HEAD TO DIRECT IT.
SINCE THIS CREATURE IS TO FLY AND NOT WALK, IT'S UNIMPORTANT WHETHER ITS LEGS ARE ALIVE OR NOT.
NOW, KEEP SILENCE WHILE I WORK THE CHARM.
WEAUGH!
TEAUGH!
PEAUGH!

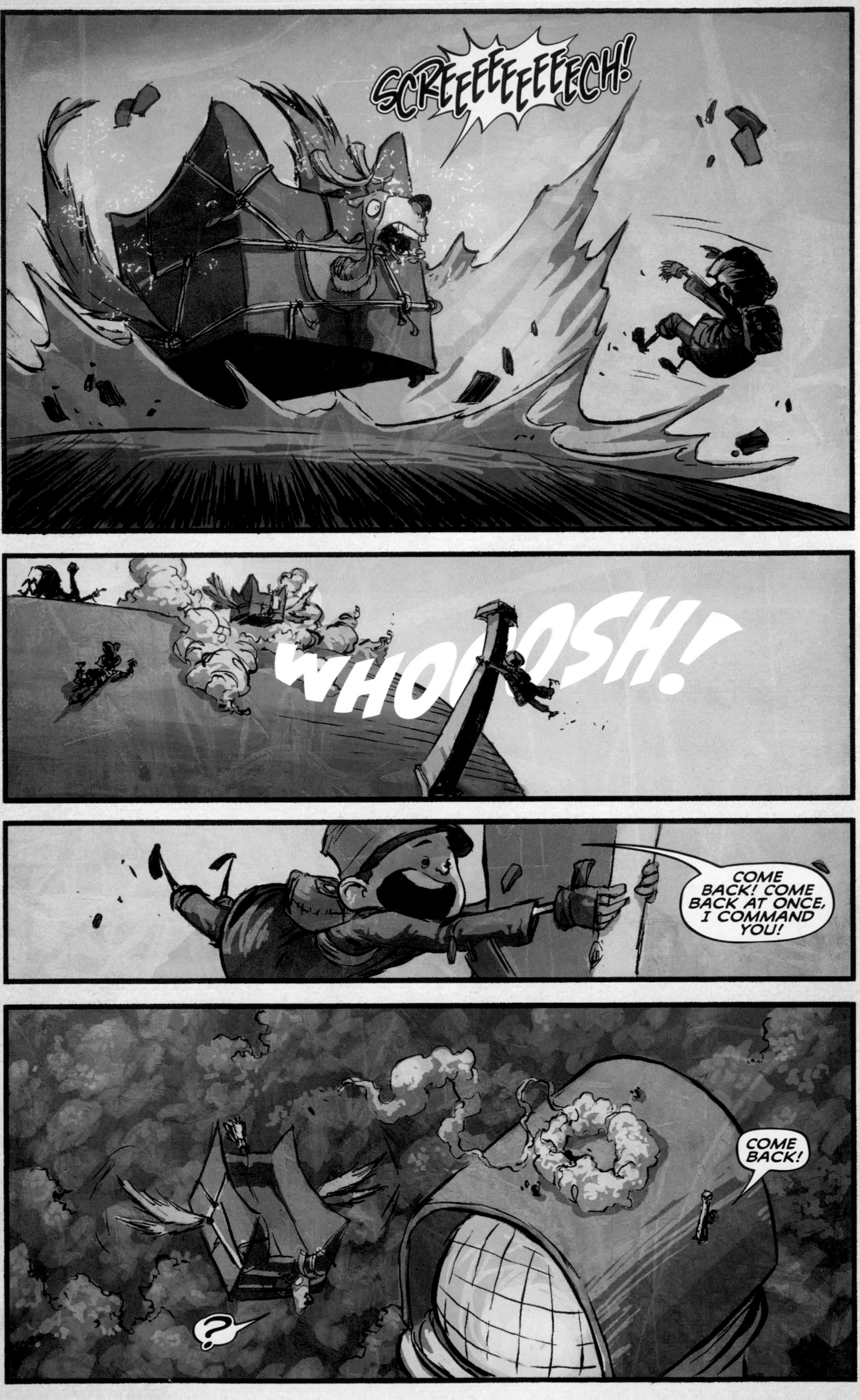
SCREEEEEEEEECH!
WHOOOOSH!
COME BACK! COME BACK AT ONCE, I COMMAND YOU!
COME BACK!
?

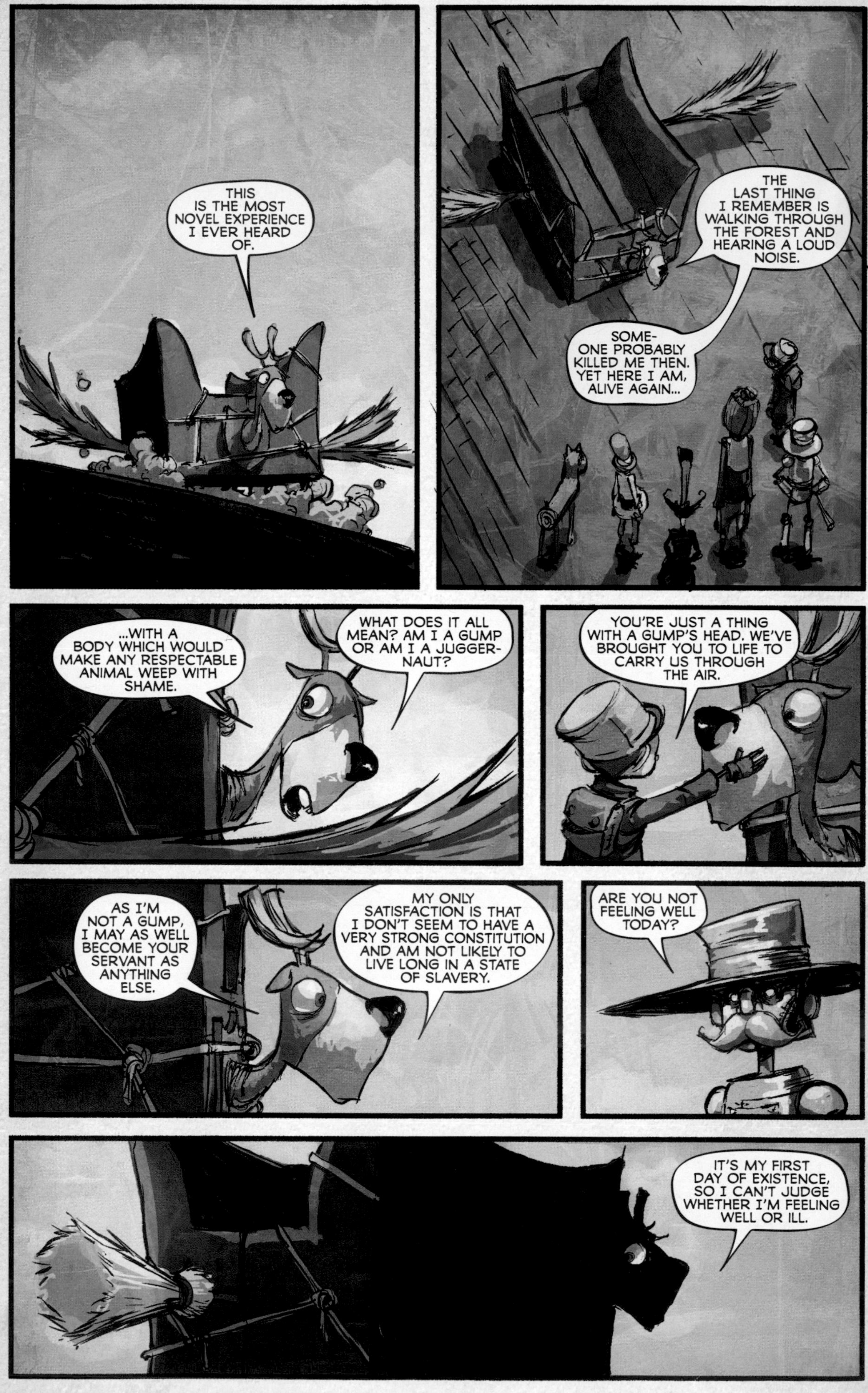
THIS IS THE MOST NOVEL EXPERIENCE I EVER HEARD OF.
THE LAST THING I REMEMBER IS WALKING THROUGH THE FOREST AND HEARING A LOUD NOISE.
SOME-ONE PROBABLY KILLED ME THEN. YET HERE I AM, ALIVE AGAIN...
...WITH A BODY WHICH WOULD MAKE ANY RESPECTABLE ANIMAL WEEP WITH SHAME.
WHAT DOES IT ALL MEAN? AM I A GUMP OR AM I A JUGGER-NAUT?
YOU'RE JUST A THING WITH A GUMP'S HEAD. WE'VE BROUGHT YOU TO LIFE TO CARRY US THROUGH THE AIR.
AS I'M NOT A GUMP, I MAY AS WELL BECOME YOUR SERVANT AS ANYTHING ELSE.
MY ONLY SATISFACTION IS THAT I DON'T SEEM TO HAVE A VERY STRONG CONSTITUTION AND AM NOT LIKELY TO LIVE LONG IN A STATE OF SLAVERY.
ARE YOU NOT FEELING WELL TODAY?
IT'S MY FIRST DAY OF EXISTENCE, SO I CAN'T JUDGE WHETHER I'M FEELING WELL OR ILL.

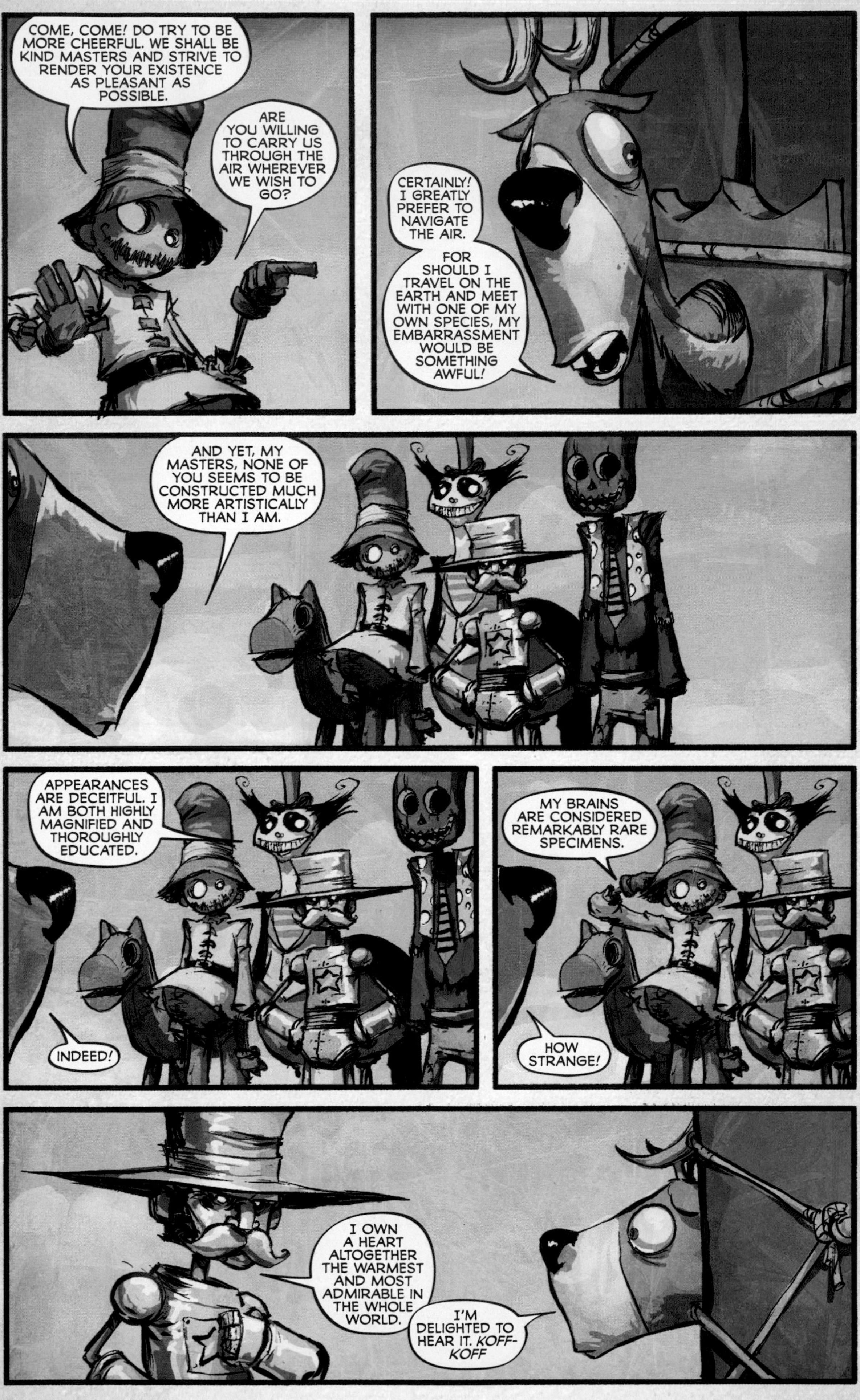
COME, COME! DO TRY TO BE MORE CHEERFUL. WE SHALL BE KIND MASTERS AND STRIVE TO RENDER YOUR EXISTENCE AS PLEASANT AS POSSIBLE.
ARE YOU WILLING TO CARRY US THROUGH THE AIR WHEREVER WE WISH TO GO?
CERTAINLY! I GREATLY PREFER TO NAVIGATE THE AIR.
FOR SHOULD I TRAVEL ON THE EARTH AND MEET WITH ONE OF MY OWN SPECIES, MY EMBARRASSMENT WOULD BE SOMETHING AWFUL!
AND YET, MY MASTERS, NONE OF YOU SEEMS TO BE CONSTRUCTED MUCH MORE ARTISTICALLY THAN I AM.
APPEARANCES ARE DECEITFUL. I AM BOTH HIGHLY MAGNIFIED AND THOROUGHLY EDUCATED.
INDEED!
MY BRAINS ARE CONSIDERED REMARKABLY RARE SPECIMENS.
HOW STRANGE!
I OWN A HEART ALTOGETHER THE WARMEST AND MOST ADMIRABLE IN THE WHOLE WORLD.
I'M DELIGHTED TO HEAR IT. KOFF-KOFF

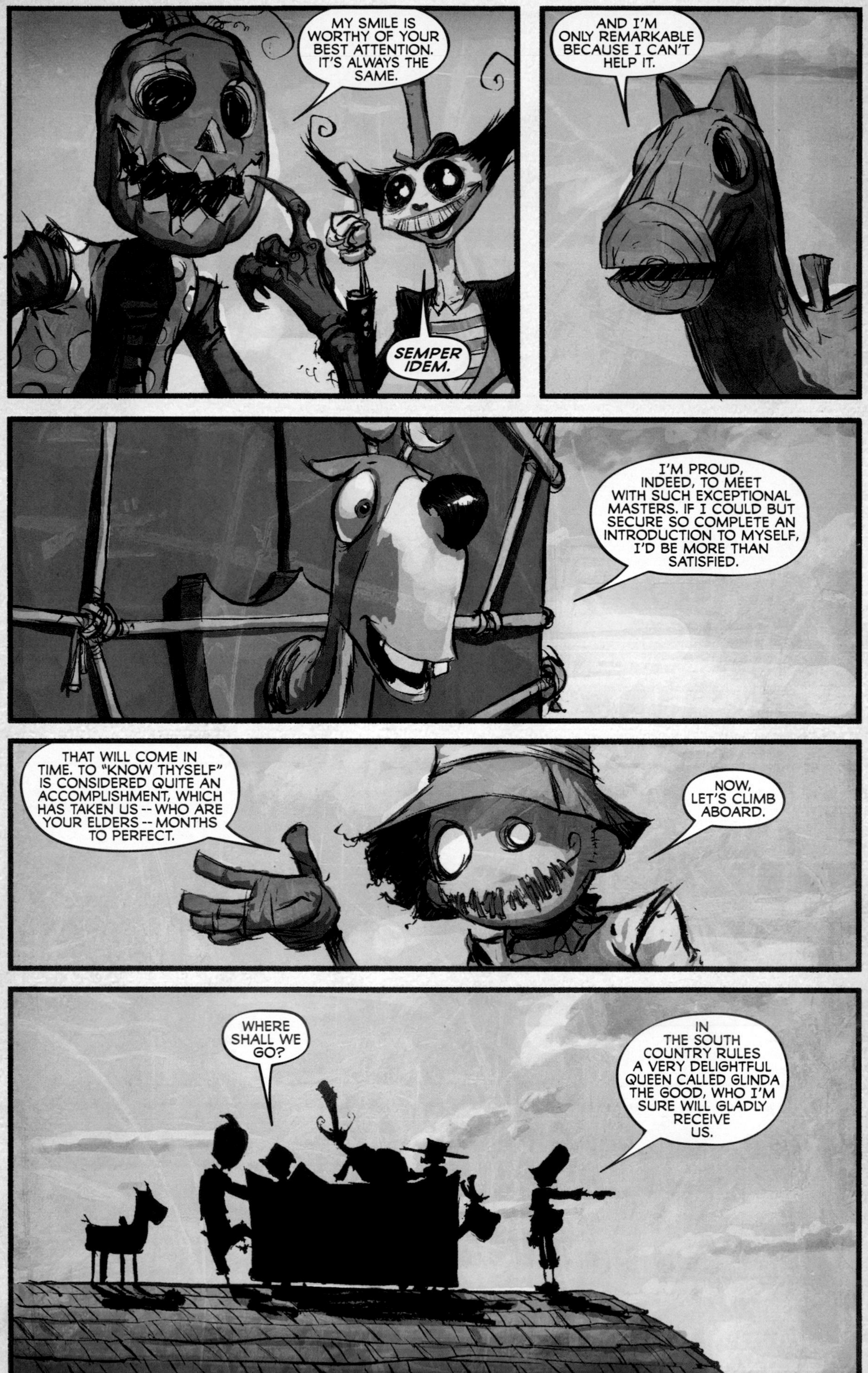
MY SMILE IS WORTHY OF YOUR BEST ATTENTION. IT'S ALWAYS THE SAME.
SEMPER IDEM.
AND I'M ONLY REMARKABLE BECAUSE I CAN'T HELP IT.
I'M PROUD, INDEED, TO MEET WITH SUCH EXCEPTIONAL MASTERS. IF I COULD BUT SECURE SO COMPLETE AN INTRODUCTION TO MYSELF, I'D BE MORE THAN SATISFIED.
THAT WILL COME IN TIME. TO "KNOW THYSELF" IS CONSIDERED QUITE AN ACCOMPLISHMENT, WHICH HAS TAKEN US -- WHO ARE YOUR ELDERS -- MONTHS TO PERFECT.
NOW, LET'S CLIMB ABOARD.
WHERE SHALL WE GO?
IN THE SOUTH COUNTRY RULES A VERY DELIGHTFUL QUEEN CALLED GLINDA THE GOOD, WHO I'M SURE WILL GLADLY RECEIVE US.

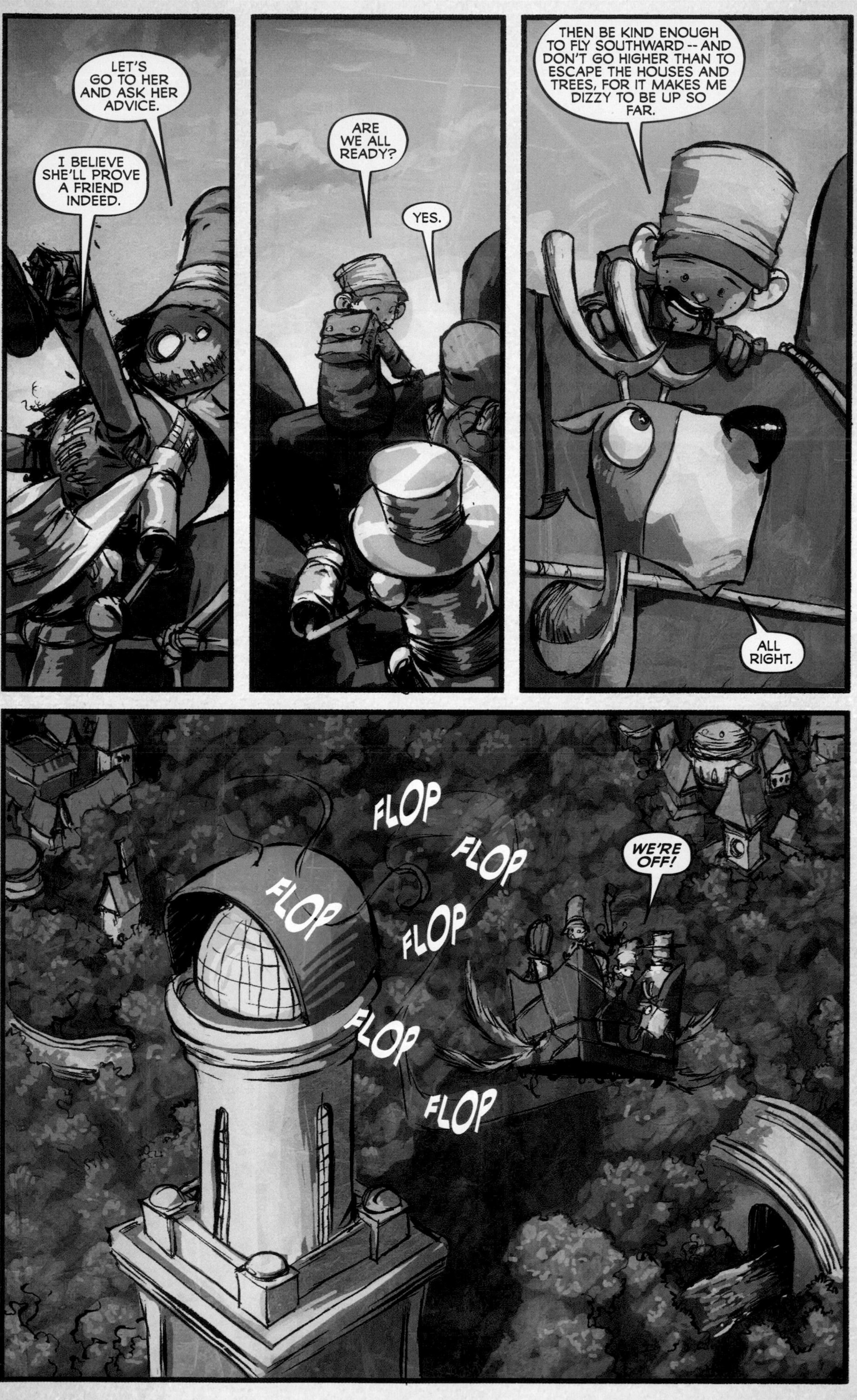
LET'S GO TO HER AND ASK HER ADVICE.
I BELIEVE SHE'LL PROVE A FRIEND INDEED.
ARE WE ALL READY?
YES.
THEN BE KIND ENOUGH TO FLY SOUTHWARD -- AND DON'T GO HIGHER THAN TO ESCAPE THE HOUSES AND TREES, FOR IT MAKES ME DIZZY TO BE UP SO FAR.
ALL RIGHT.
FLOP
FLOP
FLOP
FLOP
FLOP
FLOP
WE'RE OFF!

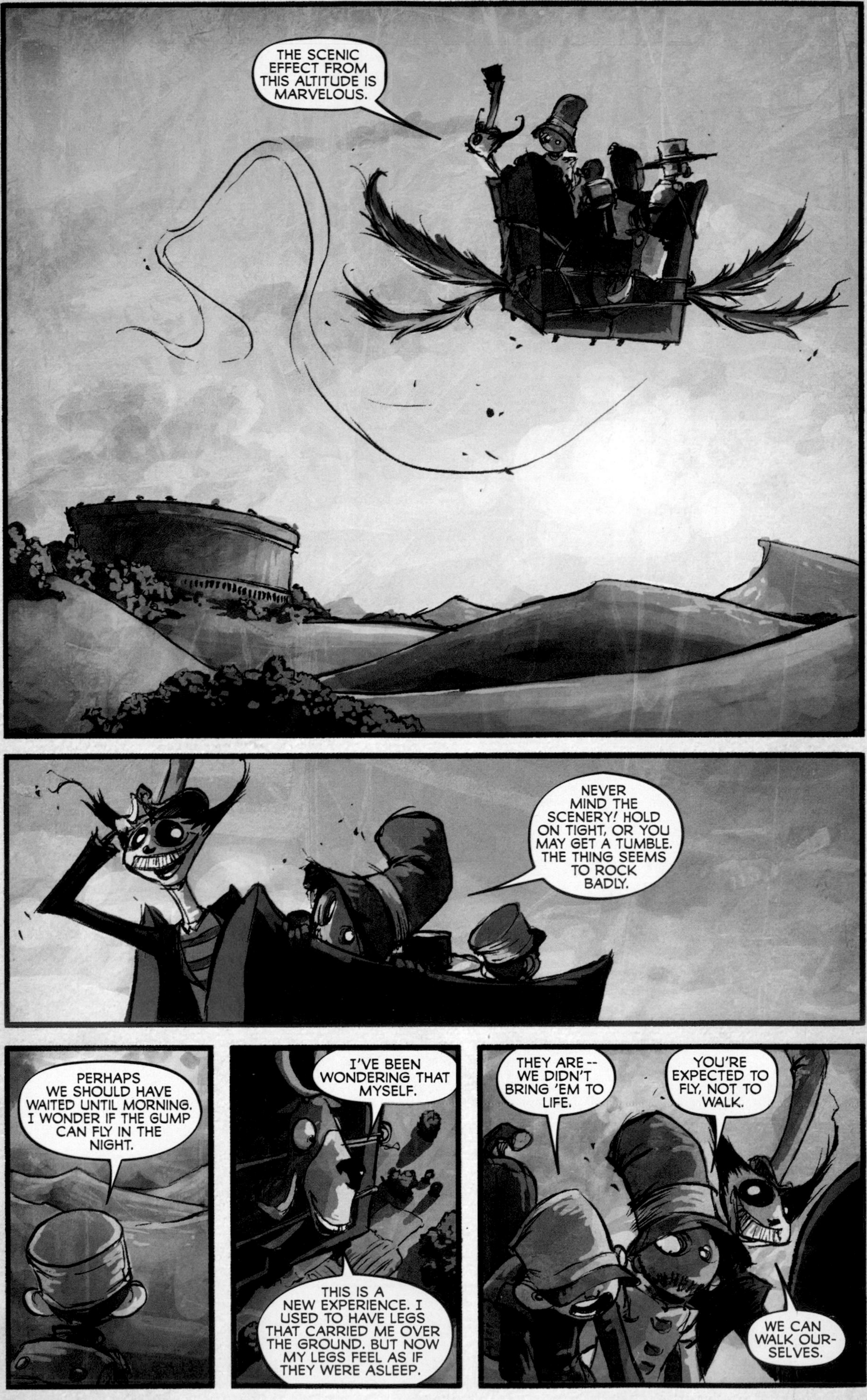
THE SCENIC EFFECT FROM THIS ALTITUDE IS MARVELOUS.
NEVER MIND THE SCENERY! HOLD ON TIGHT, OR YOU MAY GET A TUMBLE. THE THING SEEMS TO ROCK BADLY.
PERHAPS WE SHOULD HAVE WAITED UNTIL MORNING. I WONDER IF THE GUMP CAN FLY IN THE NIGHT.
I'VE BEEN WONDERING THAT MYSELF.
THIS IS A NEW EXPERIENCE. I USED TO HAVE LEGS THAT CARRIED ME OVER THE GROUND. BUT NOW MY LEGS FEEL AS IF THEY WERE ASLEEP.
THEY ARE -- WE DIDN'T BRING 'EM TO LIFE.
YOU'RE EXPECTED TO FLY, NOT TO WALK.
WE CAN WALK OUR-SELVES.

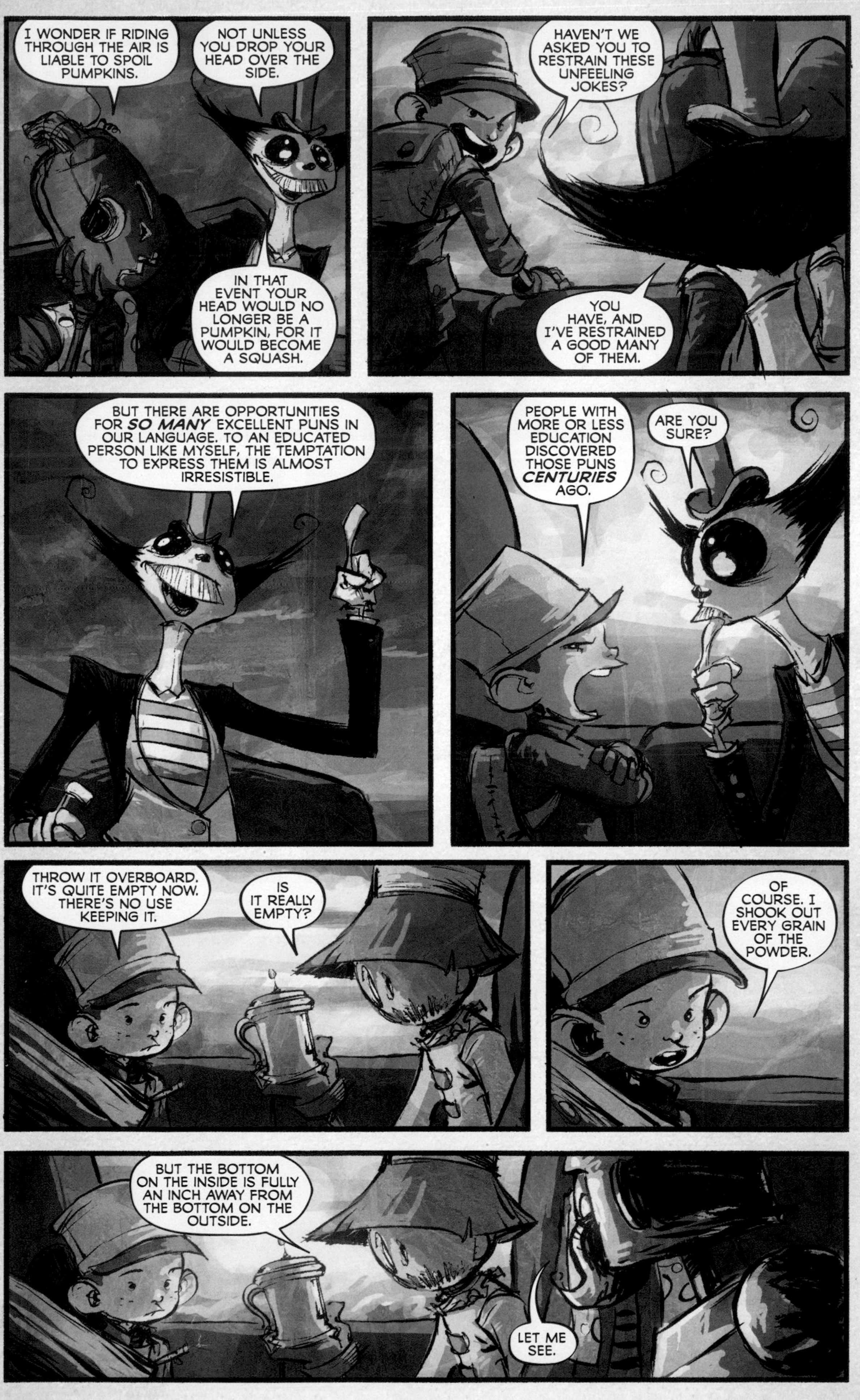
I WONDER IF RIDING THROUGH THE AIR IS LIABLE TO SPOIL PUMPKINS.
NOT UNLESS YOU DROP YOUR HEAD OVER THE SIDE.
IN THAT EVENT YOUR HEAD WOULD NO LONGER BE A PUMPKIN, FOR IT WOULD BECOME A SQUASH.
HAVEN'T WE ASKED YOU TO RESTRAIN THESE UNFEELING JOKES?
YOU HAVE, AND I'VE RESTRAINED A GOOD MANY OF THEM.
BUT THERE ARE OPPORTUNITIES FOR SO MANY EXCELLENT PUNS IN OUR LANGUAGE. TO AN EDUCATED PERSON LIKE MYSELF, THE TEMPTATION TO EXPRESS THEM IS ALMOST IRRESISTIBLE.
PEOPLE WITH MORE OR LESS EDUCATION DISCOVERED THOSE PUNS CENTURIES AGO.
ARE YOU SURE?
THROW IT OVERBOARD. IT'S QUITE EMPTY NOW. THERE'S NO USE KEEPING IT.
IS IT REALLY EMPTY?
OF COURSE. I SHOOK OUT EVERY GRAIN OF THE POWDER.
BUT THE BOTTOM ON THE INSIDE IS FULLY AN INCH AWAY FROM THE BOTTOM ON THE OUTSIDE.
LET ME SEE.

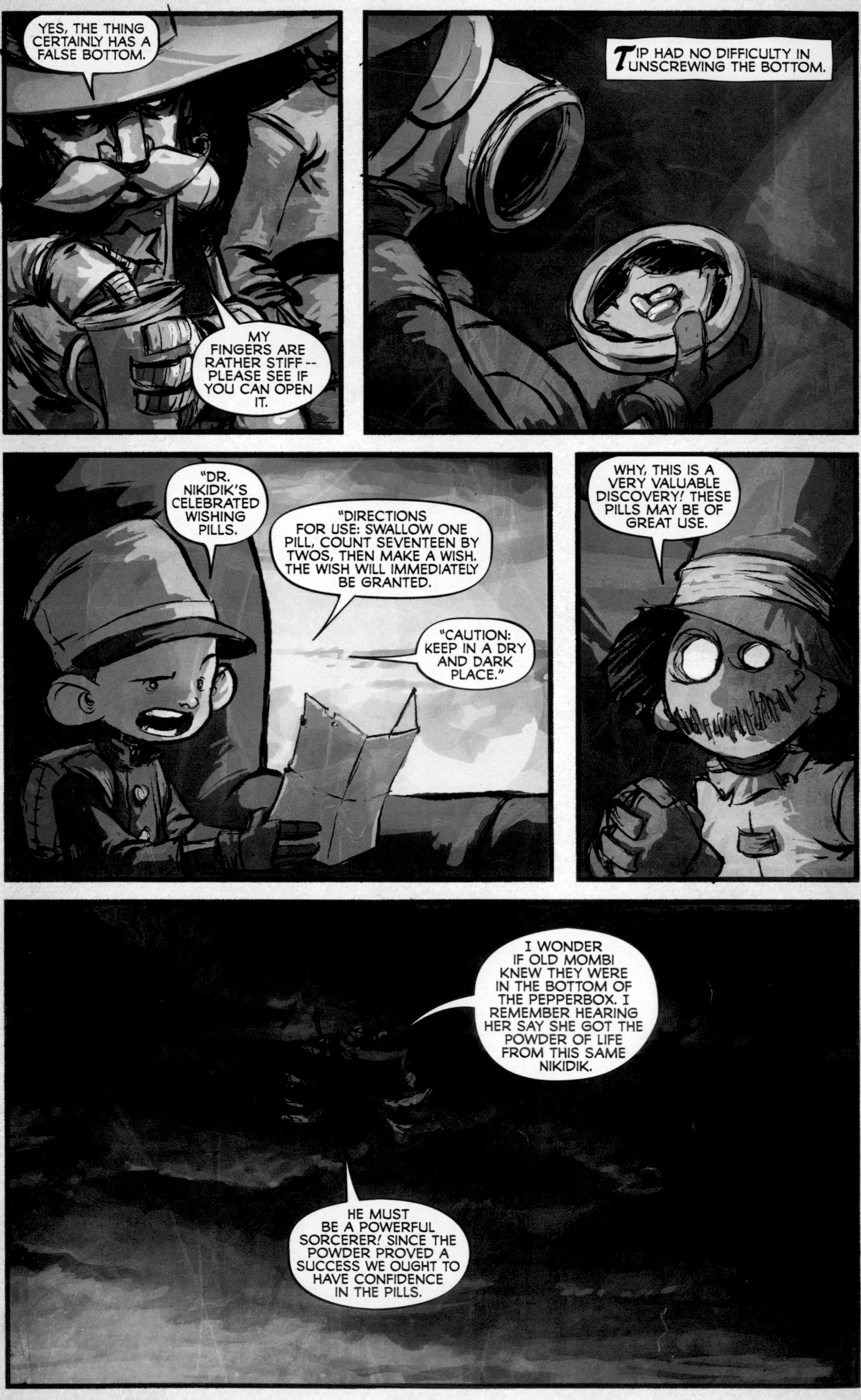
YES, THE THING CERTAINLY HAS A FALSE BOTTOM.
MY FINGERS ARE RATHER STIFF -- PLEASE SEE IF YOU CAN OPEN IT.
TIP HAD NO DIFFICULTY IN UNSCREWING THE BOTTOM.
"DR. NIKIDIK'S CELEBRATED WISHING PILLS.
"DIRECTIONS FOR USE: SWALLOW ONE PILL, COUNT SEVENTEEN BY TWOS, THEN MAKE A WISH. THE WISH WILL IMMEDIATELY BE GRANTED.
"CAUTION: KEEP IN A DRY AND DARK PLACE."
WHY, THIS IS A VERY VALUABLE DISCOVERY! THESE PILLS MAY BE OF GREAT USE.
I WONDER IF OLD MOMBI KNEW THEY WERE IN THE BOTTOM OF THE PEPPERBOX. I REMEMBER HEARING HER SAY SHE GOT THE POWDER OF LIFE FROM THIS SAME NIKIDIK.
HE MUST BE A POWERFUL SORCERER! SINCE THE POWDER PROVED A SUCCESS WE OUGHT TO HAVE CONFIDENCE IN THE PILLS.

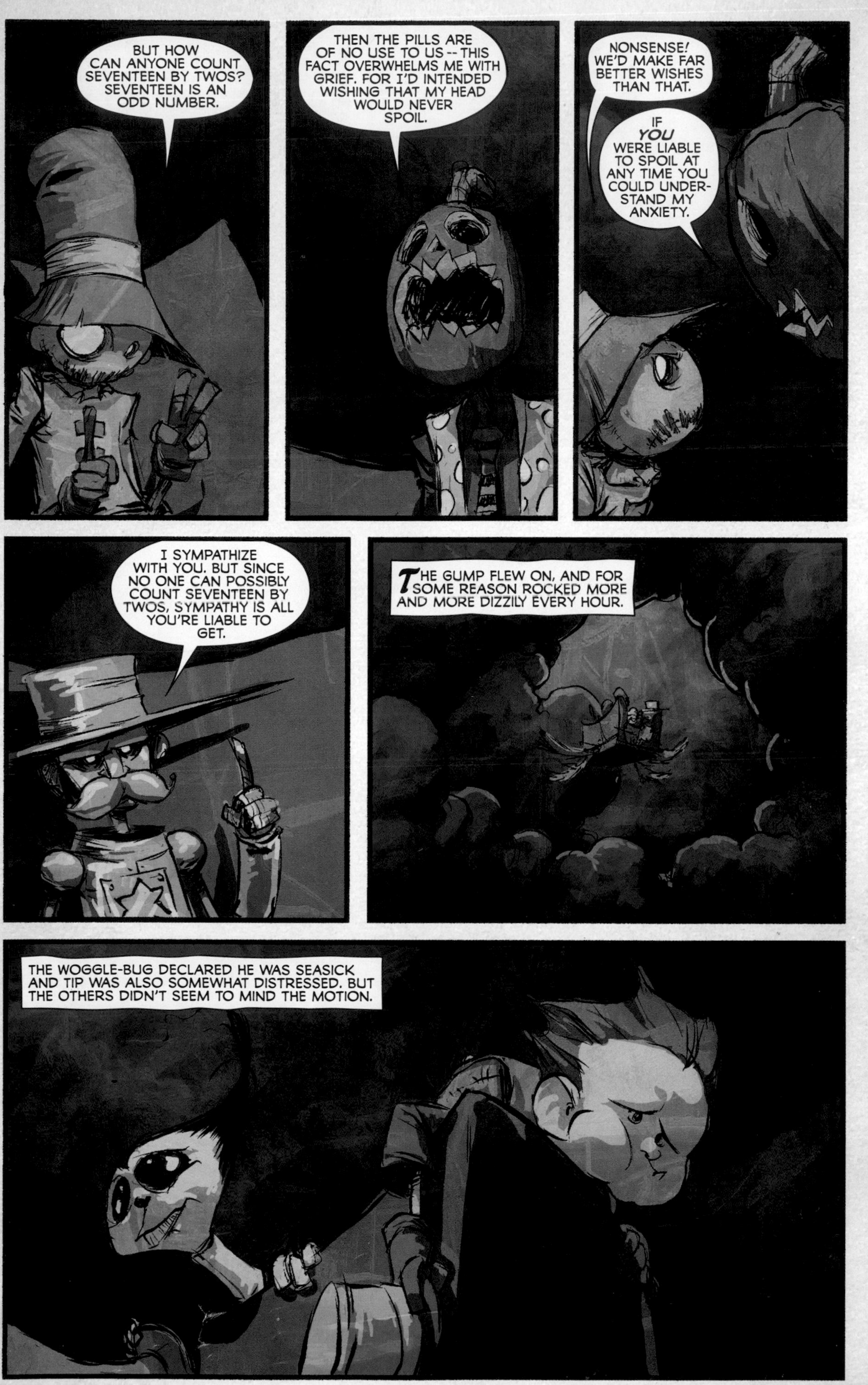
BUT HOW CAN ANYONE COUNT SEVENTEEN BY TWOS? SEVENTEEN IS AN ODD NUMBER.
THEN THE PILLS ARE OF NO USE TO US -- THIS FACT OVERWHELMS ME WITH GRIEF. FOR I'D INTENDED WISHING THAT MY HEAD WOULD NEVER SPOIL.
NONSENSE! WE'D MAKE FAR BETTER WISHES THAN THAT.
IF *YOU* WERE LIABLE TO SPOIL AT ANY TIME YOU COULD UNDER-STAND MY ANXIETY.
I SYMPATHIZE WITH YOU. BUT SINCE NO ONE CAN POSSIBLY COUNT SEVENTEEN BY TWOS, SYMPATHY IS ALL YOU'RE LIABLE TO GET.
THE GUMP FLEW ON, AND FOR SOME REASON ROCKED MORE AND MORE DIZZILY EVERY HOUR.
THE WOGGLE-BUG DECLARED HE WAS SEASICK AND TIP WAS ALSO SOMEWHAT DISTRESSED. BUT THE OTHERS DIDN'T SEEM TO MIND THE MOTION.

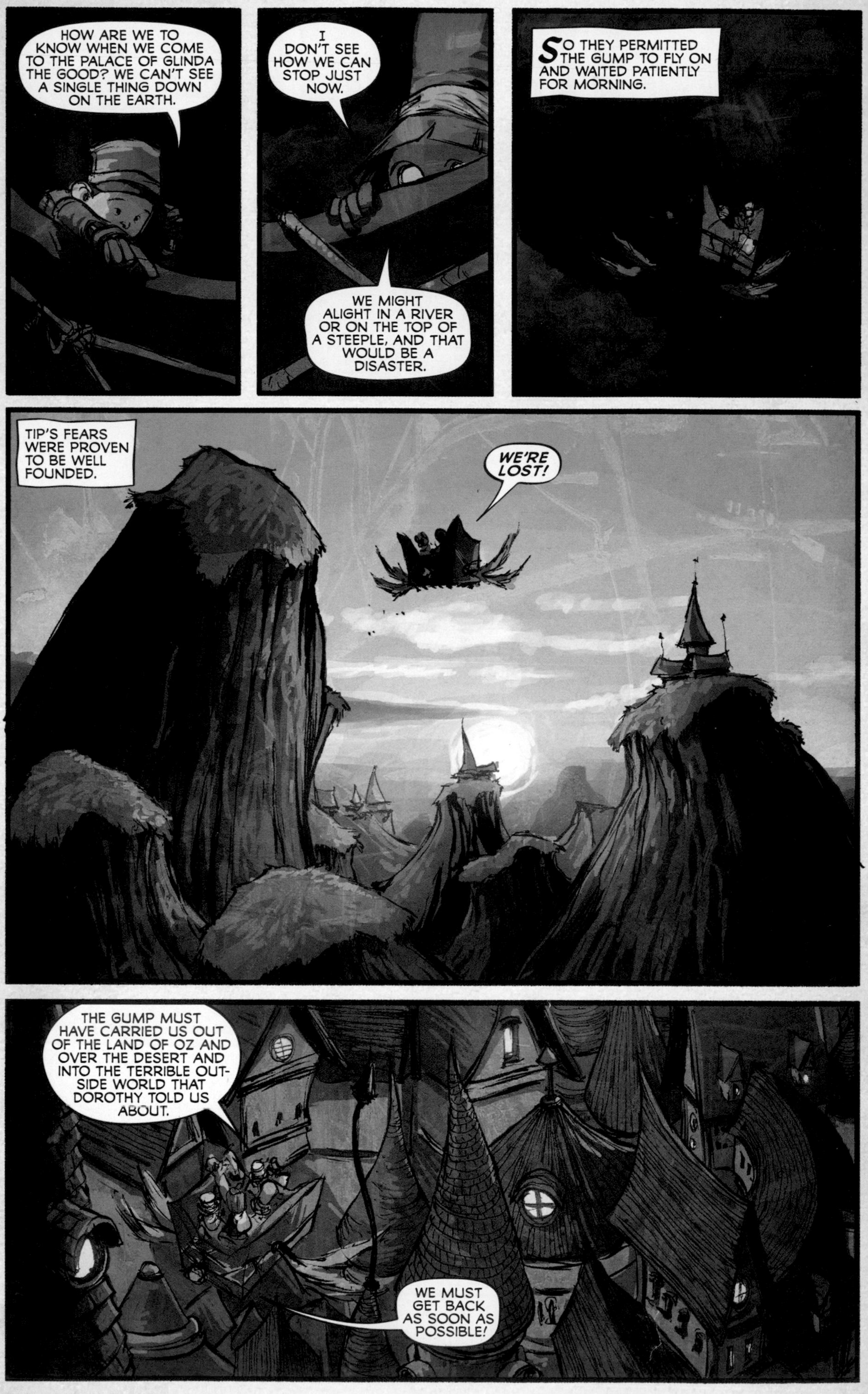
HOW ARE WE TO KNOW WHEN WE COME TO THE PALACE OF GLINDA THE GOOD? WE CAN'T SEE A SINGLE THING DOWN ON THE EARTH.
I DON'T SEE HOW WE CAN STOP JUST NOW.
WE MIGHT ALIGHT IN A RIVER OR ON THE TOP OF A STEEPLE, AND THAT WOULD BE A DISASTER.
SO THEY PERMITTED THE GUMP TO FLY ON AND WAITED PATIENTLY FOR MORNING.
TIP'S FEARS WERE PROVEN TO BE WELL FOUNDED.
WE'RE LOST!
THE GUMP MUST HAVE CARRIED US OUT OF THE LAND OF OZ AND OVER THE DESERT AND INTO THE TERRIBLE OUT-SIDE WORLD THAT DOROTHY TOLD US ABOUT.
WE MUST GET BACK AS SOON AS POSSIBLE!

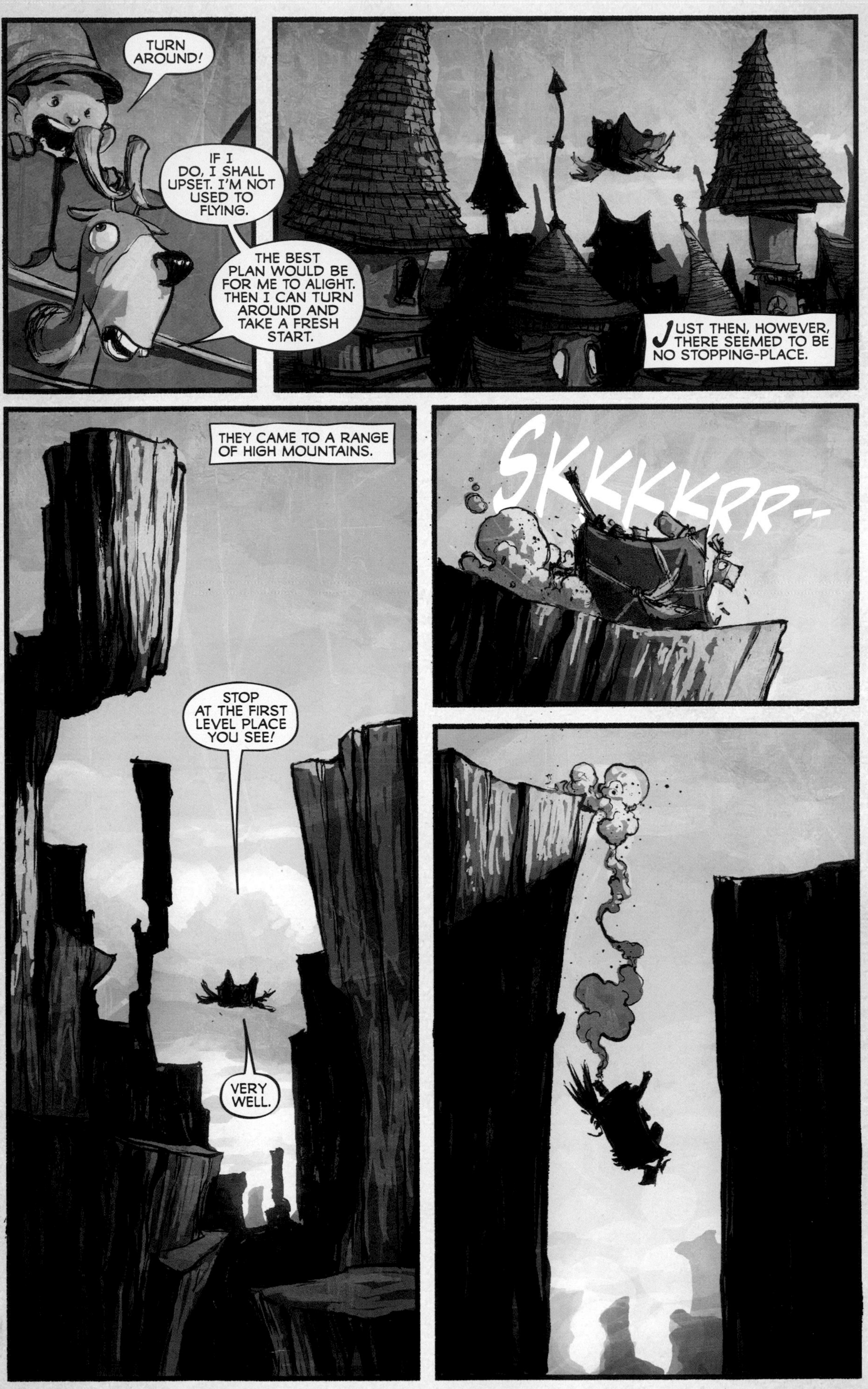
TURN AROUND!
IF I DO, I SHALL UPSET. I'M NOT USED TO FLYING.
THE BEST PLAN WOULD BE FOR ME TO ALIGHT. THEN I CAN TURN AROUND AND TAKE A FRESH START.
JUST THEN, HOWEVER, THERE SEEMED TO BE NO STOPPING-PLACE.
THEY CAME TO A RANGE OF HIGH MOUNTAINS.
STOP AT THE FIRST LEVEL PLACE YOU SEE!
VERY WELL.
SKKKKRR--

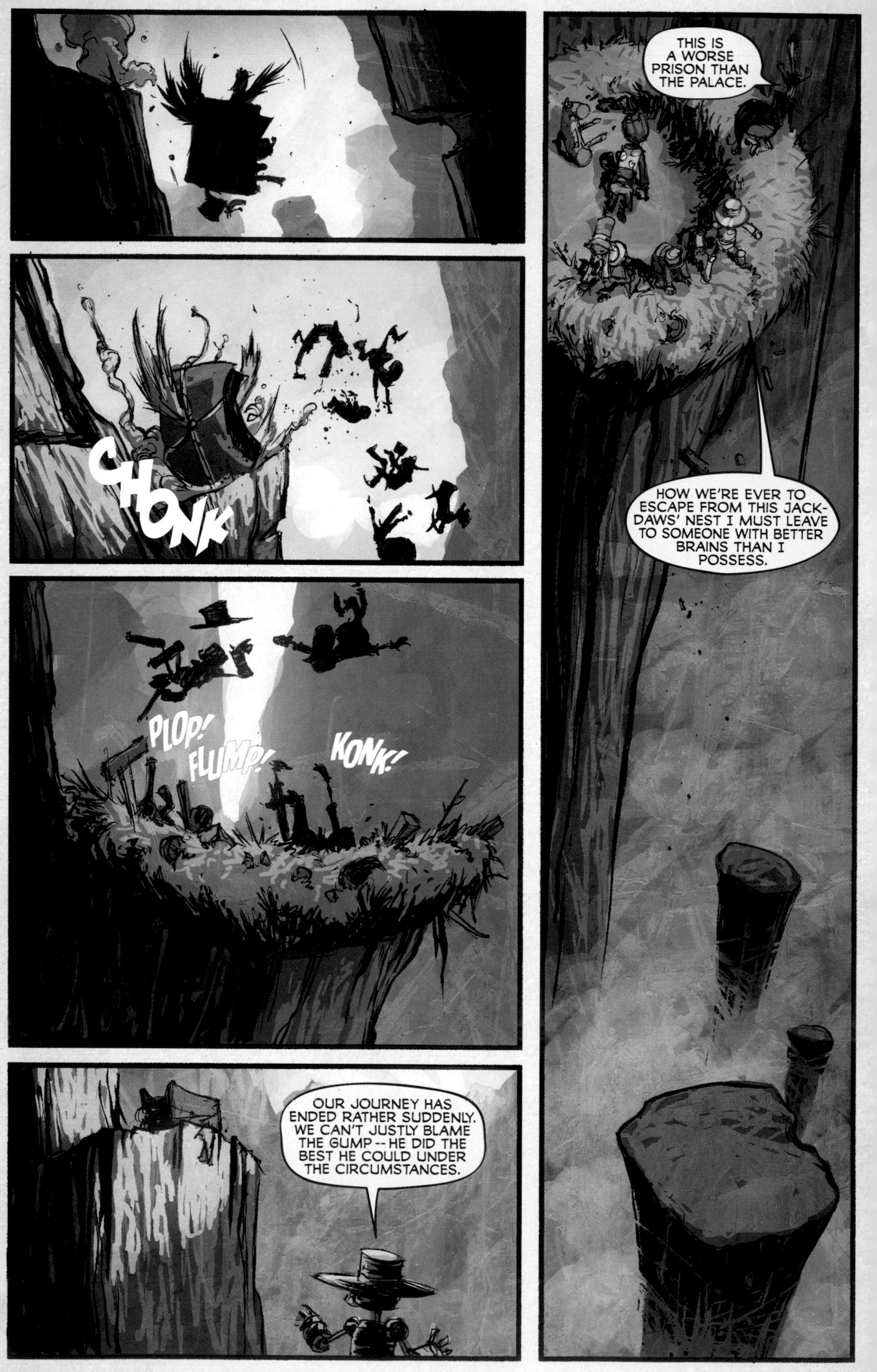
CHONK
PLOP!
FLUMP!
KONK!
OUR JOURNEY HAS ENDED RATHER SUDDENLY. WE CAN'T JUSTLY BLAME THE GUMP -- HE DID THE BEST HE COULD UNDER THE CIRCUMSTANCES.
THIS IS A WORSE PRISON THAN THE PALACE.
HOW WE'RE EVER TO ESCAPE FROM THIS JACK-DAWS' NEST I MUST LEAVE TO SOMEONE WITH BETTER BRAINS THAN I POSSESS.

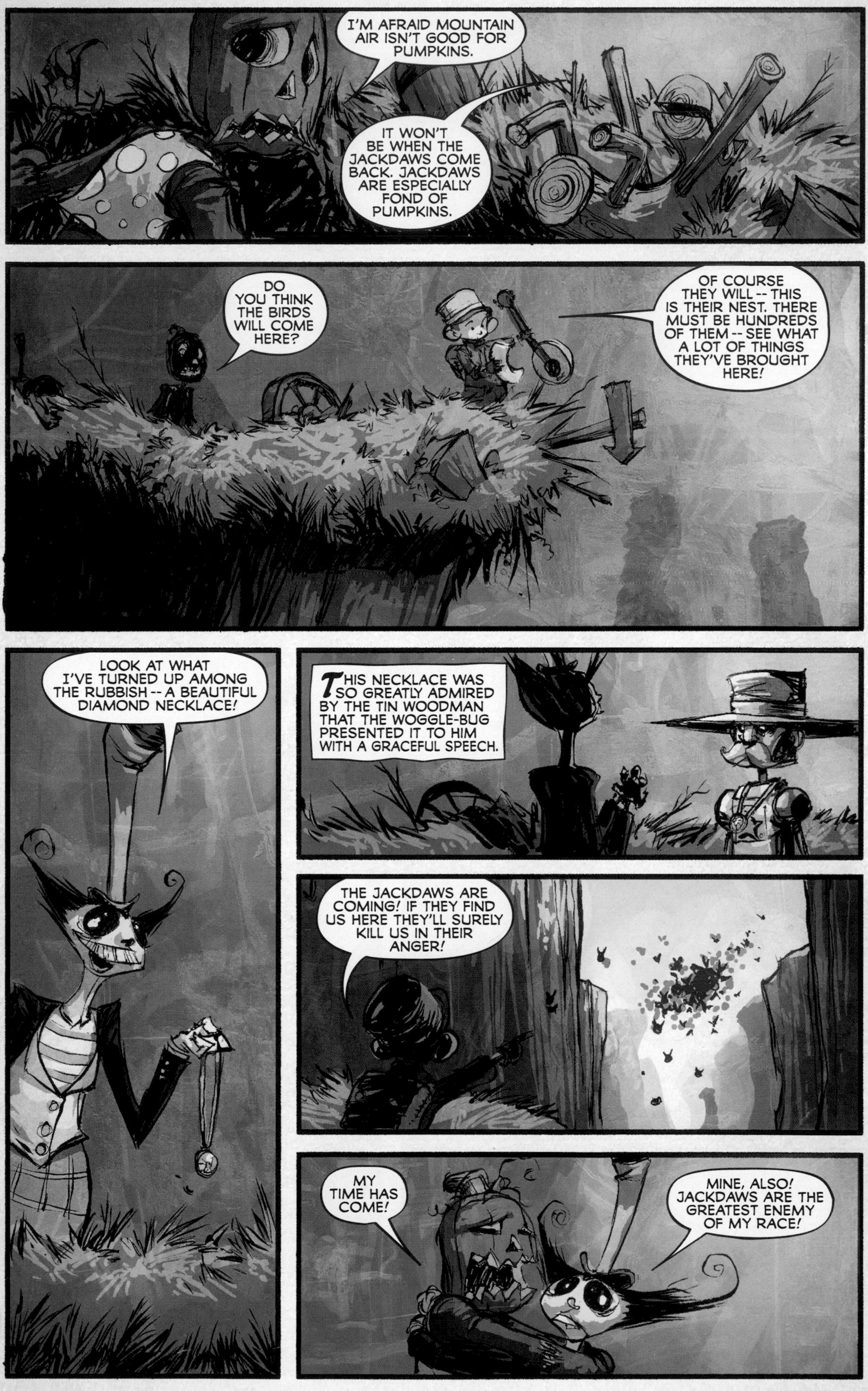
I'M AFRAID MOUNTAIN AIR ISN'T GOOD FOR PUMPKINS.
IT WON'T BE WHEN THE JACKDAWS COME BACK. JACKDAWS ARE ESPECIALLY FOND OF PUMPKINS.
DO YOU THINK THE BIRDS WILL COME HERE?
OF COURSE THEY WILL -- THIS IS THEIR NEST. THERE MUST BE HUNDREDS OF THEM -- SEE WHAT A LOT OF THINGS THEY'VE BROUGHT HERE!
LOOK AT WHAT I'VE TURNED UP AMONG THE RUBBISH -- A BEAUTIFUL DIAMOND NECKLACE!
THIS NECKLACE WAS SO GREATLY ADMIRED BY THE TIN WOODMAN THAT THE WOGGLE-BUG PRESENTED IT TO HIM WITH A GRACEFUL SPEECH.
THE JACKDAWS ARE COMING! IF THEY FIND US HERE THEY'LL SURELY KILL US IN THEIR ANGER!
MY TIME HAS COME!
MINE, ALSO! JACKDAWS ARE THE GREATEST ENEMY OF MY RACE!

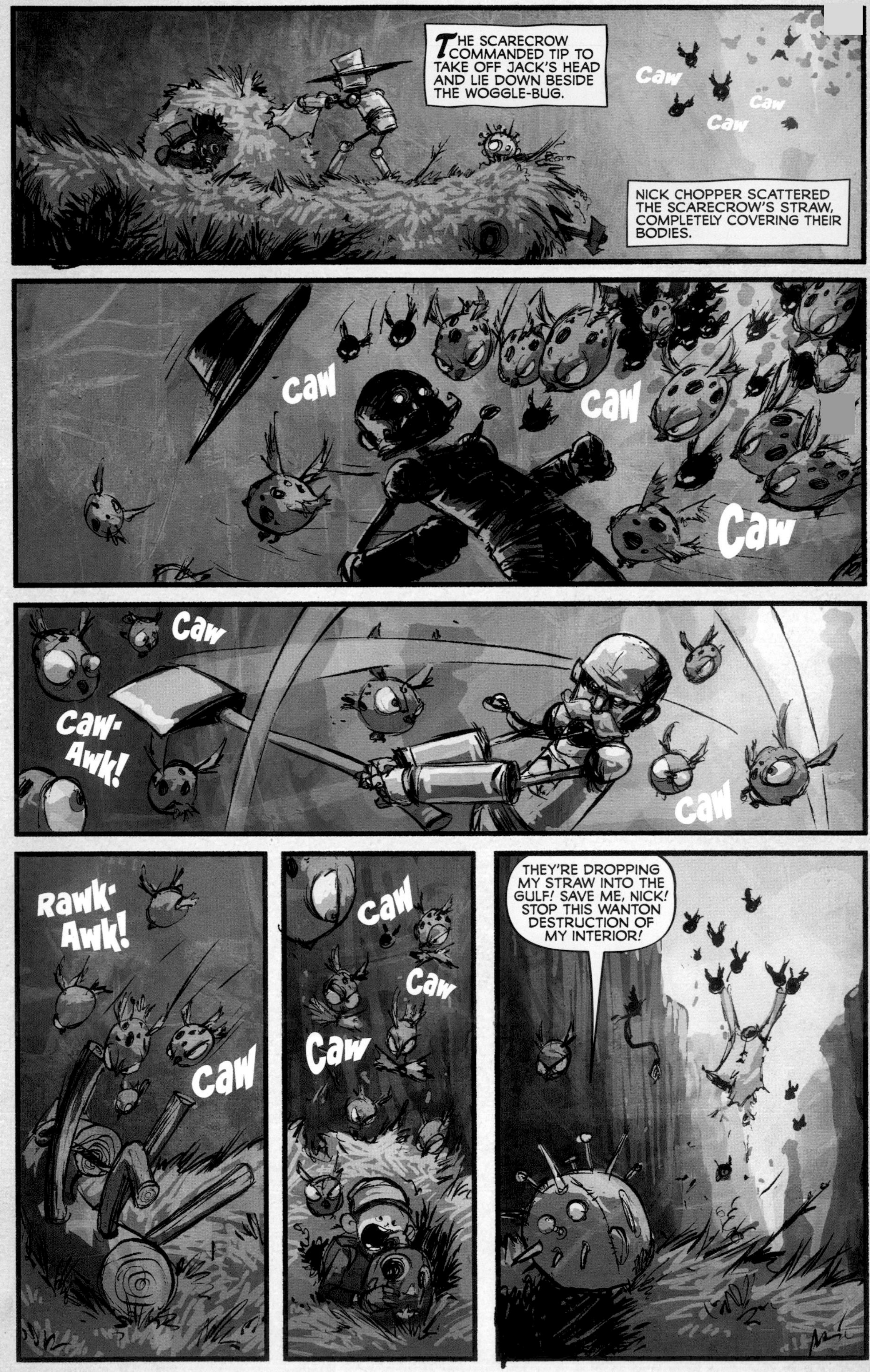
THE SCARECROW COMMANDED TIP TO TAKE OFF JACK'S HEAD AND LIE DOWN BESIDE THE WOGGLE-BUG.
Caw
Caw
Caw
NICK CHOPPER SCATTERED THE SCARECROW'S STRAW, COMPLETELY COVERING THEIR BODIES.
Caw
Caw
Caw
Caw
Caw-Awk!
Caw
Rawk-Awk!
Caw
Caw
Caw
Caw
THEY'RE DROPPING MY STRAW INTO THE GULF! SAVE ME, NICK! STOP THIS WANTON DESTRUCTION OF MY INTERIOR!

...WHICH FILLED THE BIRDS WITH TERROR.

GOOD THING MY EYES ARE OF GLASS AND CAN'T BE INJURED.

caw

caw

caw

caw

*T*HE GUMP BEGAN FLOPPING ITS REMAINING WINGS...

AS THEY FLED, THE GUMP'S EXERTIONS FREED IT FROM THE ROCK.

WE'RE SAVED!

WE ARE, INDEED!

WE OWE IT ALL TO THE FLOPPING OF THE THING AND THE GOOD AXE OF THE WOODMAN!

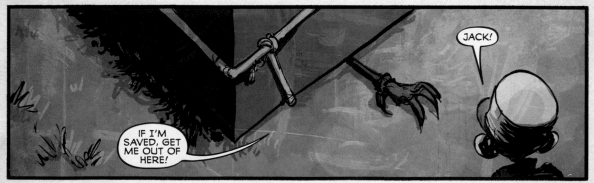

JACK!

IF I'M SAVED, GET ME OUT OF HERE!

TIP PLACED THE PUMPKIN UPON ITS NECK AGAIN AND SET THE SAW-HORSE UPRIGHT.

WE OWE YOU MANY THANKS FOR THE GALLANT FIGHT YOU MADE.

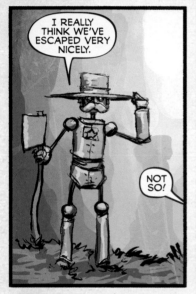

I REALLY THINK WE'VE ESCAPED VERY NICELY.

NOT SO!

I'M COMPLETELY RUINED! WHERE IS THE STRAW THAT STUFFS MY BODY? THE JACKDAWS FLUNG IT ALL INTO THE CHASM!

MY POOR FRIEND! WHOEVER COULD IMAGINE YOU'D COME TO THIS UNTIMELY END?

I DID IT TO SAVE MY FRIENDS. I'M GLAD I PERISHED IN SO NOBLE AND UNSELFISH A MANNER.

THE SCARECROW'S CLOTHING IS STILL SAFE.

WHY NOT STUFF HIM WITH MONEY?

MONEY!